For Megan

ORCHARD BOOKS
96 Leonard Street, London EC2A 4XD
*Orchard Books Australia*
32/45-51 Huntley Street, Alexandria, NSW 2015
ISBN 1 84121 894 4 (hardback)
ISBN 1 84121 280 6 (paperback)
First published in Great Britain in 2002
First paperback publication in 2003
Text and illustrations © John Butler 2002
The right of John Butler to be identified as the author and illustrator of this work has
been asserted by him in accordance with the Copyright, Designs and Patents Act, 1988.
A CIP catalogue record for this book is available from the British Library.
1 3 5 7 9 10 8 6 4 2 (hardback)
1 3 5 7 9 10 8 6 4 2 (paperback)
Printed in Singapore

# Hush Little Ones

## John Butler

ORCHARD BOOKS

Hush little ones,
you sleepyheads,
Warm and safe in
your own special beds.

Hush little rabbits, don't make a sound,

eep tight in your burrow, deep underground.

Hush little monkey,
rest your head,
As Mother climbs up to
your treetop bed.

Hush little mice, it's time to rest.

Snug in the hollow of your cosy nest.

Hush little lions, no more time for play,
Cuddle up close at the end of the day.

Hush little penguin, now you must sleep,
Nestled between your father's feet.

Hush little kangaroo, close your eyes

Drift into dreams as the moon starts to rise.

Hush little bear cubs, your bedtime is here,

Warm in your den where Mother is near.

Hush little zebra, sleep once again.

As the stars shine bright on the moonlit plain.

Hush little ducklings, curl up tight,

Snuggle together all through the night.

Hush little whale, in the deep, blue sea,

It's lullaby time for you and me.

Hush little ones,
in the silver moonlight,
It's dream time now,
goodnight, sleep tight.